MOST VALUABLE PLAYER

Also by Ruth McNally Barshaw

Ellie McDoodle: Have Pen, Will Travel

Ellie McDoodle: New Kid in School

Ellie McDoodle: Best Friends Fur-Ever

Ellie McDoodle

MOST VALUABLE PLAYER

WRITTEN AND ILLUSTRATED BY

Ruth McNally Barshaw

BLOOMSBURY

N YORK BERLIN LONDON SYDNEY

To all who do their best, who strive
to excel, and who continue to be
good sports, even when it's tough

First published in the United States of America in April 2012
by Bloomsbury Books for Young Readers
www.bloomsburykids.com

For information about permission to reproduce selections from this book, write to
Permissions, Bloomsbury BFYR, 175 Fifth Avenue, New York, New York 10010

Library of Congress Cataloging-in-Publication Data
Barshaw, Ruth McNally.
Ellie McDoodle : most valuable player / by Ruth McNally Barshaw. — 1st U.S. ed.
p.   cm.
Summary: Ellie loves the Journey of the Mind club and struggles to keep from
failing miserably on her soccer team, but when both groups have tournaments
the same day, she musters her team spirit and tries to succeed at both.
ISBN 978-1-59990-427-6 (hardcover)
[1. Teamwork (Sports)—Fiction. 2. Cooperativeness—Fiction. 3. Soccer—Fiction. 4. Clubs—Fiction.
5. Family life—Fiction. 6. Schools—Fiction.] I. Title.
PZ7.B28047Elj 2012   [Fic]—dc23   2011025797

Typeset in Casino Hand
Art created with a Sanford Uni-ball Micro pen
Book design by Yelena Safronova

Printed in the U.S.A. by Quad/Graphics, Fairfield, Pennsylvania
2 4 6 8 10 9 7 5 3 1

All papers used by Bloomsbury Publishing, Inc., are natural, recyclable products
made from wood grown in well-managed forests. The manufacturing processes
conform to the environmental regulations of the country of origin.

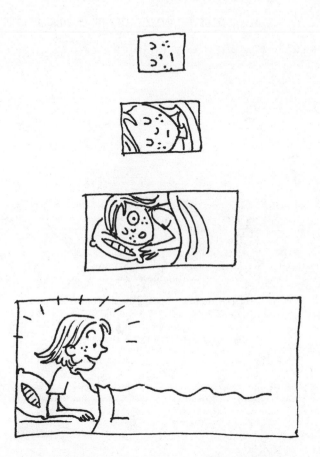

Most days, early morning slams me right back into my pillow, but today I get up happily. It's Wednesday, and that means Dad is hosting the Breakfast Games. This is his way of energizing us for the second half of the week.

Today's game is Balloon Bobble—bump the balloon into the air while eating. It's easy to keep it off the floor, but not so easy to keep it off my breakfast. My strategy is to eat FAST.

Dad, the sports nut, uses a bread loaf for a bat. The coach is coaching us: "Good job! Higher! That's it! You can do it!"

Mom, the designer, sees art in weird places: "Nice food texture and color on that balloon!"

Risa is the perfect pretty princess of power.

Josh aims most of his pranks—and the ballooon—at me.

Ben-Ben the monkey boy always wears a helmet. During Balloon Bobble that's an especially smart idea.

(Maybe I should wear one too.)

After breakfast we all scatter to school and work. I'm definitely energized.

On the school lawn, Daquon is showing us how to play Hacky Sack. He kicks the footbag to me and I flub it. Everyone groans.

When Daquon tips it, the footbag dances, dives, and soars. It won't dive for me. It only belly flops.

When the school bell rings, I try to pass-kick the footbag back to Daquon. Fail again. I pick it up and hand it to him instead.

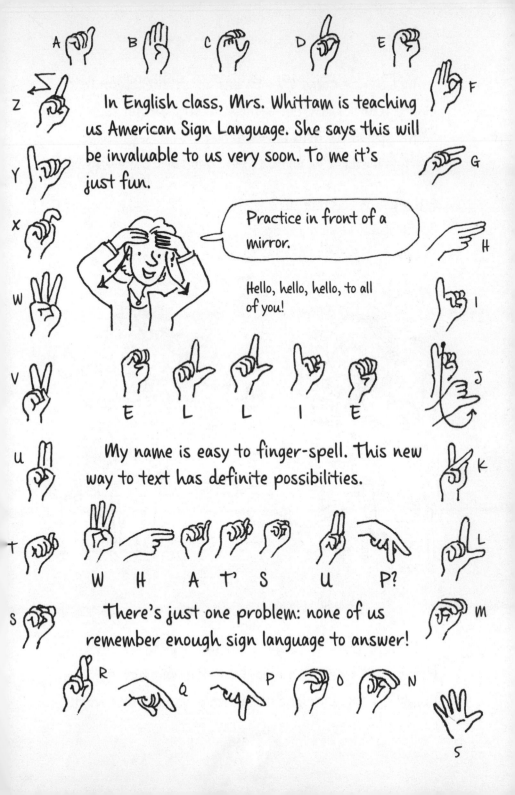

In English class, Mrs. Whittam is teaching us American Sign Language. She says this will be invaluable to us very soon. To me it's just fun.

Practice in front of a mirror.

Hello, hello, hello, to all of you!

E L L I E

My name is easy to finger-spell. This new way to text has definite possibilities.

W H A T' S U P?

There's just one problem: none of us remember enough sign language to answer!

In science class Mr. Brendall strikes fear into every heart with two words: group projects.

He splits us into small groups and separates best friends. I'm with three people I barely know.

Sitka keeps putting on lipstick and kissing papers to make lip prints

Jamian passes notes to other groups

Ahmed snores

I say, "Well, let's get started." Nobody even hears me! I decide to work on the project by myself. I LIKE science. I want a good grade in it.

After school our Journey of the Mind team meets.

What we do: Creative problem solving.

Why: It's fun! It's like gymnastics for your brain.

When: Every Monday and Wednesday.

Miss Claire hands out puzzles

The regional tournament is in three weeks. Miss Claire, our coach (and a librarian), says we have a shot at winning even though this is our first year in Journey.

Today's quick challenge: rearrange the four arrows to form five arrows. Each of us try this by ourselves.

Finally, a solution:

See the white arrow in the middle formed by negative space?

Well, I sure didn't.

Next up: another game, but this time we all have to work together. It's a team builder.

Miss Claire blindfolds each of us. Then she tells us to find the "thing" on the floor, with no hints about what it is. It isn't dust or footprints or floor tiles. (I ask.) Finally we find it: five feet of rope.

Me

Mo

Travis

Okay, that wasn't so hard. But we aren't done. While we're still blindfolded we have to form the rope into a perfect square.

This is tricky. It would be easy if I were allowed to use my T-square!

What I think we did:

What we actually did: (Pathetic!)

Miss Claire videotapes the whole process and when it's over she plays it back for us so we can see what we did right. It's eye opening. We see where a player decided not to help. Or where another player helped _too_ much.

We're good at ideas, not so good at teamwork.

Mo and I talk while packing up after Journey.

Mo: I'm trying out for the parks and rec soccer team tomorrow. You should too.

Me: Soccer? I don't know ANYthing about soccer! What if I stink?

Mo: You won't. It's easy—just kick the ball into the goal. I'll help you.

Me: We'll be too busy with Journey stuff.

Mo: The games and meetings are on different days. We can do both.

I lob objection after objection at Mo. She returns each one without breaking a sweat.

Finally, I'm out of excuses, so it's settled. Soccer, you're my game now.

When I tell Dad I'm trying out for soccer, I expect him to pat me on the head and say I'll be the best player in the league. Instead, he drops this shocker: he's the new coach!

He's taking over for a buddy who had to quit. Dad planned to ask ME to join the team!

Wait—DAD is my coach? Imagine the possibilities! He'll go easy on me. He'll practice with me. He'll be so proud of me he'll let me out of doing chores. This will be a cinch!

Me: Do I have to call you Coach McDougal?

Dad: No. You can call me Dad.

I'm so excited about soccer I can't wait to practice. I've seen soccer players heading the ball. As the star of the team, I'll need to be able to do that.

I invent my own drill:

1. Drop the ball on my head.

2. Watch which direction the ball bounces off my head.

3. Step on the ball with the foot farthest from the ball.

I drill myself over and over, fifty times in fifteen minutes.

I'll be the most valuable player, easy. With Mo and Dad on my side, I can't lose!

That night I have happy soccer dreams.

In the morning I can't wait to tell Mo the news about Dad being our coach. I kick the soccer ball all the way to school. (I admit, I'm showing off a little.)

By the time I get halfway to school my legs ache from keeping them stiff to kick.

I'm getting really good at this, though.

My on-the-way-to-school soccer practice is fantastic.

English class is going just fine.

And then the day takes a nasty turn . . .

Science stinks—literally!

Sitka's rubbing magazine perfume on her wrists. Jamian's secretly texting. Ahmed's snoring. I'm doing the work without their help.

I show my finished paper to Mr. Brendall.

Good news: I got all the answers right.

Bad news: We're also graded on how well our group worked together. A perfect score plus a terrible score equals a crummy score.

On the way home from school I kick the soccer ball extra hard (which means I'm running a lot, because that ball goes sailing all over the place).

Soccer tryouts are held at the field by the high school. Everyone's from different schools.

Dad explains that he works at the university as a coach who coaches other coaches. He hasn't played much soccer, so we'll all learn together. I hear a few groans. This pushes my protective instinct into overdrive. I scowl at the groaners.

It looks like we'll have a pretty strong team:

Danka   Hanna   Loni   Zoni

Boni   Toni   Joni   Roni   Sparkle-Sunshine

(I might have gotten some of the names wrong.)

These girls are amazing.

Everyone who tries out makes it onto the Mustangs team. Dad gets Victoria to demonstrate how to kick the ball.

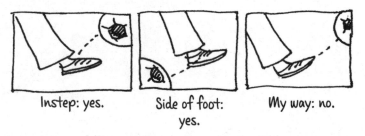

We'll have practice every day. That's a LOT of practice. I wonder if I'll get sick of soccer?

We run laps, crabwalk, and dance sideways, while kicking balls. I fall six times. My legs are pretzels!

On the way home, Dad goes into hyper-energy mode, talking loud and fast about how talented the girls are and how many games we'll win.

When I ask how he thinks I'm doing, he almost crashes into a construction barrel.

He sputters, "Good work for your first day! Keep at it! You can do it!"

Hmm. He doesn't sound convinced. And I'm not sure I am either.

In English class on Friday, Mrs. Whittam adds to our misery. "Guess what? We're doing group projects in this class too!"

Somebody whimpers. Maybe it was me.

Good news!

Our task:
1. Form groups.
2. Choose a leader.
3. Create a board game based on an ancient Greek myth.

She says our field trip to Eon Village next Monday will help with the research and brainstorming. I barely hear her, though. I'm just thinking how much I dislike group projects. I loathe them. I detest them. I 𝄒 them.

Suddenly Mo and Travis grab my arms. They claim us three as a group. This could work!

We start a brainstorming list of all the things we know about Greek mythology.

Snake-haired Medusa turns people to stone by looking at them.

Titan lord Kronos ate his own kids!

Pomegranate = apple of the gods.

Zeus is the leader of the upper world and sometimes his lightning bolt gets stolen.

Athena was born out of Zeus's head.

Poseidon is the god of the sea.

Hera is someone's wife.

Hiphisthilistithes is a god? Maybe?

Icarus had wax wings and got too bold.

    Sea: 1   Wings: 0

Gemini—wait—weren't they Roman?

Our plan: let all these names and ideas incubate for a while, and we'll talk about our game during the field trip.

This might be the first group project I ever liked. I ♡ my group!

After school I jog home, eat a quick snack, do my homework, and grab a ride with Dad to the soccer field. This will be my routine for the next six weeks.

I'm beginning to have doubts about soccer. Our first scrimmage is tomorrow and I barely understand the game. Plus, I can't keep everyone's names straight.

Mo says I'll do fine.

That night I go to bed thinking about soccer. In the morning I wake up worrying about it! What if I do something to wreck the game? Over and over? And what if everyone yells at me?

I tell Mo my fears while we kick the ball around. She comes up with a plan:

"Let's have a Mustangs sleepover! Tonight!"

It's brilliant. We'll all become best friends. Surprisingly, Dad and Mom both say it's okay. So Mo and I invite all of the girls on the team as they arrive for today's games.

Before the first game, Dad calls everyone together. He plops a box onto the bench. It's our uniforms! He tells us to take the shirt we want. Of course there's a mad scramble.

I want my lucky number. I ♡ number 3 and I always have. Unfortunately, Victoria grabs it at the same time I do. What is she thinking? I pull the sleeve and very politely inform her it's MY shirt.

Victoria pulls harder. I tell her I really, REALLY want that shirt. She puts it on and walks away. Should I tell Dad? No. This is my problem to work through. I hold my head up high and square my shoulders. I calmly walk over to Victoria and present my case.

> Victoria, that's my shirt. I claimed it first.

She ignores me.

> Victoria, I NEED that shirt. It's my lucky number. It'll help me play better.

For a second I think she's going to give it to me. But instead she wipes her NOSE on it. Cheezers. I take the last shirt in the box. It's number 29, which means nothing to me.

23

The game starts. We're the Mustangs but other animals come to mind when we play.

The Scaredy Cat
Runs away from the ball instead of toward it. Um, this is me, sort of.

The Ball Hog
Keeps the ball to herself. Refuses to share except to let someone help her score. Even then she wants all the credit.

The Chipmunk
Builds friendly chatter, encouraging everyone else. "Nice job! Keep it up! Brush it off!"

Mo is a chipmunk.

The Weasel

Accuses other players when they make a mistake. Accuses them when SHE makes a mistake too.

The Hawk

Watches, waits for an opportunity, and then swoops in and steals the ball.

We play okay, but we don't work WITH one another. We don't play as a team. Maybe tonight's sleepover will help.

We win one game and lose the other. Dad runs four victory laps and "encourages" us to also.

After the laps I walk to Mo's house to plan
the sleepover. It takes me twice as long as usual
because my legs are so rubbery.

Mo's older brother Thomas interrupts to show
me his volleyball ribbons and medals.

Thomas has Down syndrome. He
plays in Able Athletes games (sports
for kids with varying abilities). An
area meet is coming soon. Mo's mom
invites me to go with them to be an
official hugger.

Wow—all of Thomas's trophies
and medals are handmade by Mo.

Mo and I plan games and snacks for the sleepover. We want to bake cookies but Mo's mom says we should make a healthy snack. Mo tries to change her mind, but I know it's useless. Besides, it means no healthy food lectures from Dad later.

Mo and I come up with a fruit and veggie soccer girl:

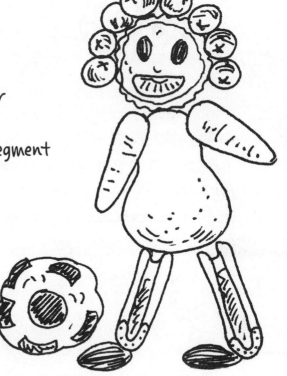

hair: blueberries
head: cracker
face: peanut butter
eyes: raisins
mouth: tangerine segment
arms: carrots
body: ½ pear
legs: celery
feet: raisins
ball: cauliflower
   with black
   olive slices

We make one for each girl. Then I go home to clean the basement for the party.

Later that night, my teammates arrive. I'm ready for them with board games, but they aren't interested. They'd rather tell ghost stories or text their friends. I don't like ghost stories.

Mo wants to play soccer outside. We try it, but seven minutes later we're back in the basement. Dad brings down two huge bowls of popcorn. As soon as he goes back upstairs, a food fight starts.

What a mess! I rush around trying to clean it up when suddenly someone screams. Then it's eleven deafening screams.

They have discovered Mrs. Claus!

We were looking for pool cues . . .

. . . and that THING jumped out of the closet!

I explain that Mrs. Claus is our family's idea of a practical joke, and that we hide her to scare one another. For fun. And it was probably Josh who hid her here. I didn't do it.

A quiet voice says, "Your family's weird."

Everyone laughs really loud.

Victoria and Loni grab cue sticks and start sword fighting.

Danka and Hanna eat the veggie girls and say they're cool. Most of the others make fun of our snacks.

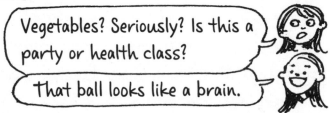

Vegetables? Seriously? Is this a party or health class?

That ball looks like a brain.

This is NOT how I was hoping the sleepover would go. We definitely aren't building any team spirit. Loni leaves early. She says she's bored.

~~Good~~ morning. Not!

Mom and Dad kept Ben-Ben out of the basement last night. But early in the morning he sneaks downstairs . . .

. . . and jumps on everyone!

Oof! Ouch! Aak! We're awake now!

It's way too early. Did I get any sleep at all? I don't think so. Half of the girls were up late talking and the other half were telling them to be quiet. And someone snores.

I'm actually glad when they all pack up and go home—except Mo. She stays to help clean up the basement, which is a HUGE mess.

We find more popcorn under the couch cushions and raisins on the bookshelves. Gross!

After we clean the basement and Mo goes home, I take a long nap. Then it's Family Night.

Sometimes we play charades or we all work on brainteasers. Tonight it's a game we invented. We call it McDougal Mayhem and it's the absolute funnest game EVER.

Board borrowed from another game. Any game. Mom and Dad made our cards.

Whenever someone lands on an agreed-upon space, in this case a chute, everyone has to pick a card from their own pile of cards. Each of us has to do what our card says. Anyone who gives a wrong answer has to go back five spaces and tell a joke. Sometimes the game can take hours.

Ben-Ben has to act out pictures:

I have to spell and define words like "stipple," "hieroglyphics," and "flying buttresses."

Josh has to identify the origin of phrases like "Veni, vidi, vici," and "Et tu, Brute?"

Risa defines music terms like "bridge," "minor," "allegro," "arpeggio," and "andante."

Mom's task is to tell what famous artist painted what masterpiece, why, and when.

Dad has to give the rules for obscure sports, like the one in England where people chase a wheel of cheese down a steep hill.

And the kicker: all the answers must be in pig Latin.

Amazingly, the final score for our game is always a six-way tie. E-way ove-lay amily-Fay ight-Nay.

Monday breakfast is entertaining, as usual.

Hello, new week!

Blueberry nutty pancakes, because you're nutty.

I ♡ when Dad wears Grandma's apron

Me: Dad, you're so corny.

Josh: Orange you glad he isn't flaky?

Mom: Dad drives me bananas.

Dad: Mom and I are quite a pear. We're already married, so we cantaloupe.

Josh: Hey—why can't you starve in a desert?

Dad: Because of all of the sand which is there! (Sandwiches. Ha!)

Today is my school field trip. Mom and Dad pack a sack lunch and give me a sandwich hug and I'm off to school.

On the bus to Eon Village I sit with the kids from the Journey team. Travis hands out puzzles.

They're from Miss Claire. She thought we'd have fun solving them before our meeting this afternoon. Fun? These are TOUGH.

What do these letters have in common?
MUYWA

All consonants? No. All have pointy parts? No. Um. I give up and ask for the second challenge.

What do these letters have in common?
BCKED

Travis, Mo, and I try to work on the puzzles but we're stumped. Instead we figure out the details for our Greek game project. We get a lot done in two hours! Mrs. Whittam winks at us.

At Eon Village it's like stepping into ancient Greece, where every myth and legend we've ever heard has come to life. Our visit starts with a history lesson. The guy talking to us can't possibly be the real Socrates, who lived almost 2,500 years ago—but he sure SEEMS like the real thing.

I only know that I know nothing.

The unexamined life is not worth living.

Wisdom begins in wonder.

SOCRATES

While we're exploring the grounds we discover monsters! They seem pretty real too!

Hungry minotaur

Plato said: "Courage is knowing what not to fear!"

A fun kind of scared

Our class splits into three groups. At the Parthenon field, one group tries out some ancient sports. Soccer was played in ancient Greece and it's still popular there today.

The winners get wreaths made from olive leaves. Mo says she's giving hers to Thomas.

My group attends the Greek theater workshop. We make masks and learn how to wear a toga.

Meanwhile, the third group learns how to make Mediterranean food. Best field trip EVER.

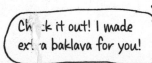

Check it out! I made extra baklava for you!

On the bus ride home everyone falls asleep, leaving me alone with my sketch journal. I learned how to give a soliloquy today. A soliloquy is sort of a speech you say out loud, but to yourself. It was fun, and who knows? Maybe I'll try being on stage someday.

My soliloquy was about sports and where they fit into my life. Dad says certain body types are best for certain sports, and it's just the luck of birth that decides what you have.

What sport is my body best for? Competitive cartooning? Marathon journaling?

As soon as we stumble off the bus (half awake) we head to the Journey meeting. Miss Claire asks if any of us solved the puzzle on the bus. (I didn't.) She gives us the answers:

They're symmetrical. When you cut these letters in half side to side, both halves look the same. (There are other letters besides M, U, Y, W, V, and A that are vertically symmetrical, but limiting it to these few makes the puzzle seem harder.)

M
U
Y
W
V
A

If you cut these letters in half this way, they look the same on the top as on the bottom. It's symmetry again. Now it seems so obvious! Why didn't we get this right before?

More brain power—pour it on!

Bonus: Which letters are symmetrical BOTH ways, side to side and also top to bottom? We think of four.

Turn the page for the answer.

Before we leave, Miss Claire hands out bags of odds and ends for a take-home project. We each get:

paper bag

three straws

two cups

three sheets of plain paper

two nuts and bolts

string

six thumbtacks

balloon

five index cards

two Popsicle sticks

pencil

tape

sponge

three washers

foam board

We have two days to make a toy using only these materials. We can use tools like hammers, scissors, hole punches, and rulers. I have no idea what to make.

Answer to bonus question on page 39: O, X, H, I

After dinner, I work on the Greek game that Travis, Mo, and I planned on the bus. I have the best job—create a game board.

When that's done I work on my Journey toy. Why is it so tough to come up with something that everyone will love playing, but is simple to make?

No great ideas come. I go outside with my soccer ball to think. Along comes the coolest dragonfly I've ever seen. He's enormous! He's perfection in flight.

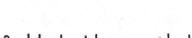

Suddenly, I have an idea!

On Tuesday morning Mrs. Whittam gives us time with our groups to finish our Greek games.

I ♡ our group. And our game!

The object of the game: Be the first to collect enough ingredients for one complete Greek myth. How we play: Roll the dice. 🎲 Move your token ♟ the number of spaces on the dice in any direction (and you can change directions at any time). Collect a card from the space your token lands on. Then it's the next player's turn.

You must collect at least one emotion card ☺, two people cards, three place cards, and four artifact cards. When you have enough cards, combine them to make up an original myth. The winner is the first to use all of his or her cards for a myth.

We play a sample game to see how it works.
I collect one emotion card,

arrogance

two people cards,

Medusa and Zeus

three place cards,

Mt. Olympus, the sea, the night sky

and four artifact
cards:

wings, wax, snakes, lightning

AND I collect some extra emotion cards:

jealousy, rage, hilarity

I only needed one of those to win. Now I have
to make up a crazy myth using all those cards.
Somehow I get through it:

Arrogant Zeus was jealous of Medusa, who made
wings out of wax so her snakes could fly her into
the night sky. In a rage, Zeus threw a lightning
bolt, which melted the wax wings. The snakes fell
into the sea and Medusa drowned. Zeus laughed so
hard he rolled down the side of Mt. Olympus.

In science class Mr. Brendall tells us to chart the life cycle of a star. Instead I chart the life cycle of our science group:

1. Nebula explosion: we begin in a cloud.

Some people in my group stay in the cloud the whole time.

2. Gravity forces some particles together.

Mr. Brendall's heavy hand forces us into groups. (All of the annoying particles repel the superior, kind, smart ones. You know, their opposites.)

Work in groups!

3. Things heat up and glow if the group works well.

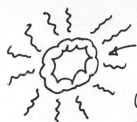 4. Energy is created.

(In our case, the energy leaves our group and goes to shine on other groups.)

5. The cloud explodes and a star is born.

If it's a huge star, it becomes a supernova and then a black hole. My group is the black hole of the class, sucking all the fun out of it.

I ask Mr. Brendall if we can switch groups now.
No.
I ask if I can be my <u>own</u> group, by myself.
No.
I ask if I can do a different project, at home.
He gives me a sit-down-and-be-quiet look.
At the end of the hour, the other groups are smiling and giving high-fives. My group is not.

After school I jog home, grab a snack, and get ready for soccer practice.

Me: What are you building?
Risa: Ick! What stinks?
Josh: Bat houses.
Me: Bat houses stink?
Risa: Your shoes do!

I spray them with Risa's perfume. It doesn't help—now they're flowery stinky.

Me: Why are you making bat houses?
Risa: What's that horrible smell??
Josh: So they'll attract bats.

I spray them with room deodorizer. Now they're Bay Breeze-ish flowery stinky. Gross!

Me: Why do we want to attract bats?
Risa: Did something die in your shoes?!
Josh: So the bats will eat the mosquitoes.

I wonder if baking soda or underarm deodorant would help. No time to try it—Dad says it's time to go.

Soccer practice is brutal. Dad has us do stretching and exercises first. I notice I only packed one shin guard. Oops.

Then we do air sits, which are harder than they look. Keep your back straight and bend your legs, like you're about to sit.

My legs wobble and burn. My face turns red. My brain feels like it's going to explode.

Next we hobble onto the field for small-group drills (and you know how I love working in small groups). My legs already burn from the air sits, now add to that some new bruises.

My unguarded shin is getting banged up pretty bad.

Joni

Victoria

Oops! Sorry!

Zoni

It's a kicking competition. And my leg is the ball!

I'm so glad when practice ends and I can ice my poor shin at home.

Dad tells me he has tickets to the women's soccer game at the university on Friday night. I get to invite four kids to go with us. I pick Mo, Travis, Daquon, and Yasmeen.

Really? That's who you want to invite?

Oh boy. It turns out that Dad wants me to invite girls from the soccer team, and he has definite opinions about which ones: Mo, Fifa, Zoni, and Victoria. I wonder if Victoria kicked me on purpose today. Sigh.

Then Risa further ruins our nice dinner by talking about her evil cat.

My kitty is an important member of our family. He needs a name.

Josh and I offer up a few suggestions:

Cat-astrophe	Calamity	Kitsch	Evil Incarnate
Disaster	Miss Chiff	Miss Take	Bratty Cat
Horrible	Terrible	Awful	Cat Forsale
Obtuse	Bleeder	Malaise	Pierce

I like Pierce because it reminds me of Peter, who gave me the kitty. But some of those other names are kind of mean.

Pierce is the perfect name for him, considering what he does to my poor legs.

After dinner I work on my moving toy for tomorrow's Journey meeting: a flying dragon.

1. Cut two wings and one head-body-tail piece out of foam board or poster board.

2. Decorate the parts.

3. Tape the wings to the body so they're in an "up" position.

4. Thread a string through a washer. Tie one end of the string to each of the wings so the washer hangs below.

5. Now loop a long string through the dragon's back for hanging (my dragon is hanging from our ceiling fan). Pull down on the washer and the wings flap down. Let go and the wings fly up.

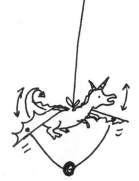

Mom admires it. Then she sends me to bed, but my brain won't go to sleep. I start thinking about the olive leaf crown at Eon Village.

It'd be neat to make a crown of stars for Thomas, for the Able Athletes meet.

I know what could work: the ninja star! It takes a lot of steps but it's not actually hard to make.

How to Make a Ninja Star

1. Start with a 4x6-inch index card. Cut two 4x1-inch strips from it.
   Two strips make one star.

Use the rest of the card to make more ninja stars!

2. Color one strip red on both sides so it's easier to follow these instructions.

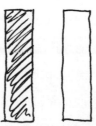

3. Fold both strips in half and then unfold.

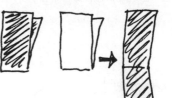

4. Fold the red strip on the dotted lines.

Now the strip looks like this:

5. Fold on the new dotted lines:
   Fold down the top (a) to make a roof shape (b).
   Then fold up the bottom (c) to make an S shape (d).

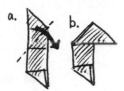

6. Repeat the steps with the white strip. Notice that the folds go in the opposite direction this time.

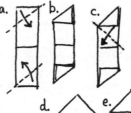

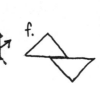

7. Flip over the red shape (only the red one).
   Rotate the white one.

52

8. Put the white shape on top of the red shape.

9. The top red corner will tuck into the white triangle on the right, and the bottom red corner will tuck into the white triangle on the left. Start with the top one:

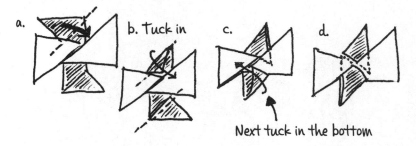

a. b. Tuck in c. d.

Next tuck in the bottom

10. Flip it over.

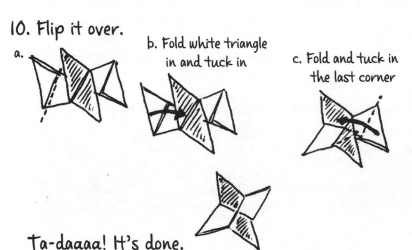

a. b. Fold white triangle in and tuck in c. Fold and tuck in the last corner

Ta-daaaa! It's done.

I make and string together a dozen stars. I'll make more tomorrow.

Good morning! Today must be Wednesday because Dad gets us up early for the Breakfast Games. We're playing No-Lose Musical Chairs. It's a little messy our way.

1. For six players, we use five chairs. Then we eat breakfast while walking around the table to the music.

2. When Dad stops the music, we all scramble for a seat.

(This works best with <u>dry</u> cereal in your bowl.)

3. We take out one chair. Now we have six players and four chairs.
4. Start the music again. Everyone walks (or dances) around the table.
5. Stop the music suddenly and—

Try to sit!

Keep taking out a chair and restarting the music. Pretty soon you'll have one chair with six players piled onto it, giggling.

Grabbing bites of breakfast in between playing the game and laughing isn't easy . . . but it's fun!

This is going to be a great day. I can't wait for my Journey meeting, where I get to show off my dragon.

That afternoon at our Journey meeting we're all excited to see what everyone made.

Kev made a boat with an inflated balloon as a motor.

Kwanita made a paper doll that dances when you stick your fingers through the leg holes in her tutu.

Bae made a pinwheel.

Glenda made a sponge puppet.

Daquon made a zip line with a miniature Miss Claire riding it.

Mo made a bird mobile.

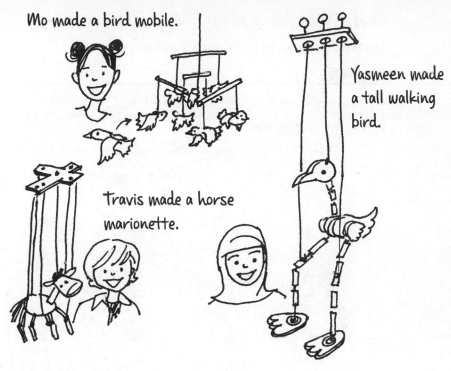

Yasmeen made a tall walking bird.

Travis made a horse marionette.

Ryan drew his mom on a card, punched holes in the shoulders, and pushed Popsicle sticks through to make arms. It's the freakiest arm-waving puppet ever.

front

back

nut and bolt lets arms pivot up and down

And I made a dragon that flies.

Soccer practice is after the Journey meeting.
I have decided soccer is a painful sport.
Evidence:

- Dad makes us do push-ups and sprints—which
  burn my muscles.

- It hurts to know I'm not good at this.

- And then there's the unique pain of knowing
  Victoria.

Victoria's question takes me by surprise. Why <u>am</u> I on the team? Do I even <u>like</u> soccer? I feel sick.

I tell Dad my stomach hurts and he lets me sit on the bench for a while.

Watching my team practice, I worry that Victoria is right. They're better without me.

I can't wait to get home, but when I do, I wish I was someplace else. Risa and Josh are shooting hoops.

"Hey, Smiley, catch!" Josh throws the ball to me.

Risa chants, "El-lie! El-lie! El-lie!"

So I shoot. I miss. I try a few more times. And then Risa and Josh start mysteriously missing their shots. I see the nods. I see the raised eyebrows. I know what they're doing. They know I stink at basketball so they're letting me win!

I don't ever want to win because someone gave me an unfair advantage. I want to win because they played their best and I played better!

That night I should be doing my homework, but I can't stop thinking about soccer and winning and losing and what is best for the team.

I make a list of things I could do:
- Work harder to be a better player (but is that even possible?).
- Quit soccer (but will Dad get upset?).
- Tell Victoria to go take a flying leap off a flying buttress (but are there any around here?).
- Accept that I will never excel at soccer. Find a different sport (but what if I stink at that too?).
- Make soccer fun (but how?).

On Thursday in English class we finally play our Greek games. Greek Gods and Goddesses Bingo and Torch Relay are too simple. Twenty Questions about Ancient Greece feels too much like homework. I'm very excited when it's time to play my group's game, It's All Greek to Me.

Mrs. Whittam is pulling off the lid, and—

Eeeek!!!

It's a paper version of Mrs. Claus! With fangs! My teacher and the class all laugh. It takes a long time to calm everyone down and explain who Mrs. Claus is and why she's in the game box—which I wonder about too. Playing my group's game isn't nearly as much fun as the Mrs. Claus discovery.

At soccer practice I avoid Victoria.

Doing the exercises, I keep up with the group and try not to complain.

Running laps, I stay in the middle of the pack. On the field, I watch the ball.

I even put away my book and pen so I can concentrate on the game.

But no matter what I do, I still stink at soccer. And I don't mean my feet, which I suspect also stink. I take a shoe off to investigate. Victoria notices and orders me to put it back on. I stick my tongue out at her. Dad happens to be watching.

This is me, running laps for showing unsportsmanlike behavior.

I guess Dad can tell I'm annoyed because we drive without talking.

We stop at a Greek restaurant. We have to wait in line for a few minutes. Awkward silence.

Finally we get a table. Dad sits where he can see every door—he calls it the power seat. I take the chair opposite the power seat. Dad scooches his chair LOUDLY all the way over to my end of the table. It sounds like a howler monkey—I think the people across the street can hear it!

He's practically in my face. Cheezers.

Over falafel sandwiches and Greek salad, Dad starts. "Okay, sport. Shoot. What's the score between you and soccer?"

I shrug.

"Ellie, we're on the same team. I can take it."

Okay, fine. I'm honest. I let it all out: I hate the exercises and I'm a lousy player and Victoria is snotty to me every single day.

Of course Dad has the right words for me. He says it's okay to dislike the exercises or be mad at my coach and my teammates. And nobody is perfect at a new sport.

He asks if soccer is even a little bit fun. I have to think for a few minutes before saying yes.

A funny thing happens. I don't really need Dad's permission to quit the Mustangs. And he doesn't exactly give it. But I get the sense that it'd be okay to quit.

At home Dad and I kick the soccer ball around. It's pure fun, until the rain starts.

That night as I'm drifting off to sleep, thunder pounds around me. The room brightens with each lightning strike. I'm not afraid, though. I feel safe and warm, protected by the roof above. And by Dad. I decide to stay on the team.

Rrrumble

Ker-ASH!

Zzzzz

Goodnight, Ophelia, my sweet rat.

In the morning the world is swampy.

I loved the rain when I was little. I hopped in every puddle, soaking my clothes.

Today I jump <u>over</u> puddles. When you run in the rain, do you get wetter because you crash into more raindrops? Or do you stay drier because you run between the raindrops? I'm not sure, so I run half of the way to school and walk the other half. I could have swum to school and stayed drier.

At lunch we have to stay inside because it's still raining. A group of us play Finger Football.

How to Make a Finger Football

1. Fold a page of notebook paper in half vertically.

2. Fold in half vertically once more.

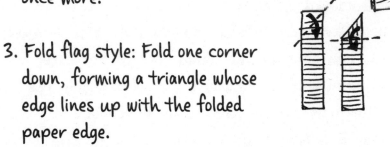

3. Fold flag style: Fold one corner down, forming a triangle whose edge lines up with the folded paper edge.

Continue folding the paper to create triangles until there is not enough paper left for another triangle. Keep the folds tight.

When you have just a little "tail" left (a), tuck it into the previous fold (b).

How to Play Finger Football

1. In one turn, Player A flicks the triangle football across the desk toward Player B.

   To score a six-point touchdown, the football must stop on the desk with a corner hanging slightly over Player B's edge of the desk.
2. After scoring the touchdown, Player A can try for the extra point. To get the extra point, Player A must then position the football at the halfway point on the desk, and flick the football through Player B's upright goalpost fingers.

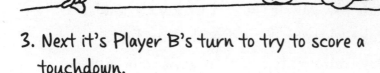

3. Next it's Player B's turn to try to score a touchdown.

Variation:
* Try to score a touchdown in three flicks instead of just one.

Mo and I make up goofy cheers for Finger Football that we perform with our hands.

Rah-rah ringer, kick it with your finger!
Rah-rah rum, kick it with your thumb!
Rah-rah rail, kick it with your nail!
Rah-rah ruckle, kick it with your knuckle!
I think I should come up with cheers for our soccer team.

Rah-rah rankle, kick it with your ankle.
Rah-rah root, kick it with your foot.
Rah-rah rinstep, kick it with your instep.
Rah-rah red, hit it with your head.
Okay, so it needs work. I'm not giving up on the idea, though.

At the end of the day Principal Ping's voice comes over the intercom to announce that next week is Spirit Week. Five days of fun stuff to build school spirit.

Mo: Next week is the best week of the year.

Me: Because of Spirit Week?

Travis: Did you forget?

Me: Ooooh. (big eyes at Mo)

Travis: Ha! Some best friend YOU are!

Me: Quiet, Travis! Mo—

Travis: A BEST friend would remember!

(Mo: smiling the whole time)

Me: I didn't forget.

Travis: I bet you also forgot that the Party Games are at my house this weekend.

Me: Oh!

Travis: You forgot that TOO! Well, remind your family. And don't bring Mrs. Claus.

All the way home from school I'm thinking I seriously need to do something special for Mo's birthday next week!

It's no longer raining. Soccer practice is on. There is more dirt than grass on our field, so today the field is a giant mud pie. We're sliding around, sloshing through it, sending out mud spray every time we kick the ball.

And the ball isn't that easy to kick. Sometimes it sticks to the ground.

Victoria has a new nickname: Mudslide. Maybe I laugh a little too loud and long at that.

I'm not the only one who thinks it's funny, though. Everyone is laughing. We're all a sopping, gooey mess.

If soccer were always this fun, I would never dream of quitting!

The university women's soccer game is tonight. I wonder how well they'll play in the mud?

Mo, Fifa, Zoni, and Mudslide (aka Victoria) arrive at my house all cleaned up and dressed in university colors for the soccer game. Mom insists on taking a photo of us.

Fifa   Zoni   me   Mo   Victoria

We cram ourselves like a pack of clowns into a van and head to the arena. On the way, we entertain Dad by singing the university fight song over and over. First normal, then loud, then quiet, then with British accents, then French, then surfer dude, then Southern belle, then Martian . . .

We can sing lots of versions because we're stuck in traffic. Dad tries a different route, but it doesn't help. It just gives us more time to sing.

The game is
SO COOL!!!

They have cheerleaders! They have GUY
cheerleaders! There's a band! There's a huge
audience—and they sing the songs and cheers.
Mo, Mudslide, and I write down all of the words.
We want to teach the rest of our team so we can
make our games more fun.

And then there's the players! They're AWESOME! They run a LOT. It's actually fun to watch them. Just being here I feel like I'm a better player already.

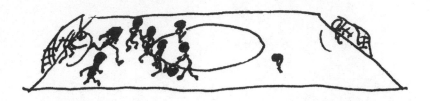

Fifa and Zoni spend most of the game standing in the hallway buying stuff. What a waste of two tickets. I could have brought Travis or Daquon instead!

Mo invites Mudslide to the Able Athletes meet but Mudslide says she was already planning to go.
I'm getting along okay with Mudslide, but that doesn't mean I want to see her at every event in my life.

At the end of the game Dad brings us down to the field (where there's no mud, by the way) to meet the players.

I ask my favorite player how she dribbles the ball so well.

Practice.

How much practice? I tell her I've been trying almost nonstop for a week.

She says, "Keep at it. Every month you'll see improvement."

Months?? I was hoping for hours. Or minutes.

Going to the game tonight made me want to try harder to love soccer. We have two games tomorrow and then Party Games at Travis's house at night. I'm trying not to think of Party Games as the reward after a long day of punishment (soccer games).

After tucking in my soccer ball and thinking only kind thoughts about the Mustangs, I make a few more stars for Thomas's crown.

Star tally: 19.

That gets me thinking: what should I do for Mo's birthday next Friday?

Saturday morning I wake up still thinking about Mo's birthday present. In a momentary lapse of good judgment, I ask Risa for ideas.

"Get her some perfume."

Mo isn't a girly girl.

"Cute hair clips."

She doesn't use hair clips. She makes two ponytails into messy buns. No clips.

"Get her a book on hairstyles. She's ignoring the whole wide world of fashion."

So, make her feel like her hair isn't good enough just the way it is?

As if on cue, Josh comes in.

Josh: The fashion industry thrives because women aren't good enough.

Me: Josh, you're outnumbered two to one, so you might want to rephrase that.

Josh: Get Mo the thing you want the most.

Me: What I want? Why?

Josh: So you can borrow it. And maybe she'll re-gift it to you!

Me: No.

Josh: Get her what I want. A goat.

Me: No.

Josh: A blanket with sleeves.

Me: No. Three strikes. You're out.

Risa: You want to get her something truly fabulous? Get her a kitty.

Me: No. I LIKE Mo. Why would I get her an instrument of torture?

Risa: Get her a soccer bracelet to wear during the games.

Me: You can't wear soccer bracelets in games!

Just then Dad comes in and shares some creepy stories about sports injuries caused by girls' bracelets, rings, and necklaces.

Risa and Josh want to hear all the gory details. I do not. Besides, it's time to get ready for my game. I make sure I have both of my shin guards (no replay of Shin Bruise Day).

My shoes are still a little damp from yesterday. They really, <u>really</u> stink.

I shake a clump of baby powder into each shoe and shove my feet in.

A puffy white cloud poofs around my ankles, leaving my socks, shoes, shorts, and the floor dusty white (and smelling like foot stink plus baby powder).

Something occurs to me: if babies actually smelled like this, it would quickly bring an end to the human race.

I try to brush away the powder. It makes me cough, it spreads farther, and it does NOT wipe off easily from my clothes. Cheezers.

I arrive at the soccer field with baby powdery feet. Every time I take a step a little cloud flies up. I run behind everyone so nobody notices.

Dad puts us through the usual warm-up routine. I'm stretching every body part I have—and a few I didn't know about.

The other team's bus arrives. The players come bounding off the bus like graceful gazelles. Their uniforms are cool. There's no powder puffing from anyone's feet.

They huddle together and one player yells, "Auggie, Auggie, Auggie!"

The others yell, "Oi, Oi, Oi!"

I have no idea what that means but it makes my knees weak. They're so confident, it's scary!

Our team's families arrive. To our embarrassment, they're carrying pom-poms. And COWBELLS. Now I'm really nervous.

Josh brought his friends Iggy and Doof, and his friends brought kazoos. They're watching the game closely, cheering at the right times, and playing songs.

Of course everyone notices them.

Especially the girls on my team.

Hanna, Boni, and Sparkle are fixing their hair on the field. They're tucking in their shirts and adjusting their shin guards while checking out Josh, Iggy, and Doof. Roni is putting on lipstick. It's sickening watching them primp and flirt. Josh is my brother! Not some cute guy!

I get to play a little in the beginning of the first game, and I make a couple mistakes.

1. I pass the ball to Joni and it's intercepted by the other team. I should have aimed at Mudslide, who was closer. And open. Oops. The other side scores on my mistake.

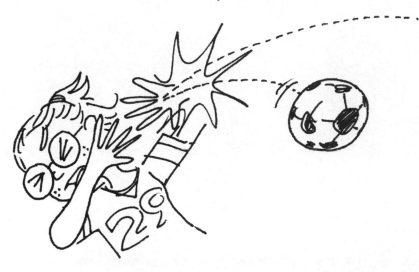

2. One time the ball comes toward my face and instinctively I throw my hands up to protect myself. Immediate whistle blow—HANDS!—and a penalty kick for our opponents. To my horror, they score AGAIN, off my foul. I'm close enough to Dad to hear him mutter:

Aw, sugar beets!

I'm thinking things can't get any worse, but then they do. I'm kicking the ball and my shoe goes sailing off my foot and into the air. It slaps against Mudslide's leg.

Someone on the other team says to me, "Nice shot, Shoe-fly."

As the game progresses I hear Dad in the background, gradually getting louder. First the mutter, now he's shouting bad words.

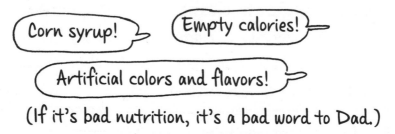

Corn syrup!

Empty calories!

Artificial colors and flavors!

(If it's bad nutrition, it's a bad word to Dad.)

Some of the parents pick up on the bad words and invent new ones. They read their candy labels and pick out ingredients to yell when someone on the field makes a mistake.

> Oh, partially hydrogenated vegetable oil!

> Emulsifier!

> Resinous glaze!

My mom and her friends are really into the game. They're waving their pom-poms and chanting cheers from thirty years ago. And they're waving their cowbells, which clang REALLY loud, every time someone does something right.

They can't save the clanging for when we score, because we only score once.

The dads are crazy too. Roni's dad is running up and down the sidelines, yelling encouragement to just her. He's her own personal cheering section.

> Go, Roni! You can do it! Keep your eye on the ball!

We lose the first game 5 to 1. Dad gives us a pep talk: Focus on the next game. You know how to win it. You can beat them. Don't let your guard down. Pay attention on the field.

We go into the second game pumped up and ready to win. Five minutes later the score is 0 to 0. All of the players are clustered at the Mustang goal. Half are fighting to get the ball into the goal and the other half are fighting to keep it out.

I'm playing hard. I'm playing to win. I am determined to score, no matter what it takes.

A weird thing happens. I DO score . . .

Fifa kicks the ball to me. It bounces off my shin. I don't actually kick it. I want to be clear on that.

So the ball rolls into the goal and scores. What I mean is, it bounces off of me and into OUR goal. The OTHER team scores. Off me!

They dance and scream and laugh. They yell, "Thanks, Shoe-fly!"

My team circles me. I hear things like, "It's okay," and "It could have happened to anyone," and "This isn't your day, huh?"

Mo hugs me. She says, "Shake it off."

Roni calls me a comedy of errors. Maybe one day I'll laugh at this, but that day isn't here yet. We lose the second game 4 to 3. We lose by one point—my point.

Because we lost both games we have to run laps—like we're not already feeling punished enough.

Halfway through the third lap, Loni starts running toward the equipment pile. She grabs her bag and walks to her mom's car. She gets in, and they drive away.

This is NOT a good time to quit. We're just starting out! She should give us a chance.

The team divides into those who think it's rotten of Loni to leave now and those who wish they had the guts to leave also.

Everyone's arguing. I'm glad to go home.

I get home to find Josh and Risa packing camp chairs. I almost forgot (again)! It's party time!

The Party Games are a four-family tradition we just started. One evening a month Mo's family, Travis's family, Iggy's family, and my family meet at one house and play games.

The little kids play simple board games. The grownups play complicated stuff like bridge and mah-jongg (from China).

The rest of us play anything fun. It's sort of a challenge among the families to see who can bring the funnest game.

Travis's dad takes this challenge VERY seriously. He actually researches to find award-winning games before anyone else does. To this we say, "Game on!"

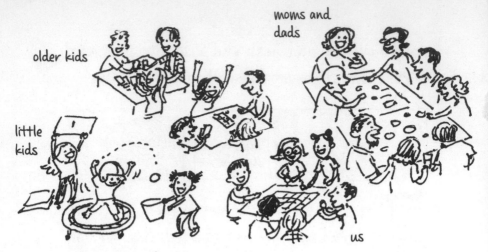

older kids

moms and dads

little kids

us

As some of the games end, the groups remix and new games start.

At one point we're making a house of cards. Whichever team makes it fall has to get up in the middle of the party and hula dance for 60 seconds. Travis makes it fall.

Ohhh nooooo!!! Travis is on my team! This is NOT good.

camera

None of the other groups know why Travis and I are dancing the hula. They just think it's hilarious. And of course they all grab cameras. The video will live on forever, I know it.

In response to our humiliation, Travis teaches us how to play Smoke, Smoke, Fire:

One player holds up the deck of cards with one card showing at a time.

If it's a black card ♣♠, the other player says, "Smoke," and a new card is shown.

If it's a red card ♦♥, the other player says, "Fire."

That's all Travis tells us. He demonstrates on Mo, showing her five cards in sequence.

Smoke.
Smoke.
Smoke.
Smoke.
Fire.

"Fire? Okay!"

Next comes 52 Pickup (picking up the 52 cards). We all help.

Party Games night runs past the little kids' bedtime. Before we want to, we're packing up to go home.

At home I count the stars I've made for Thomas's crown. Thirty-seven, and I wanted a hundred. Able Athletes is tomorrow!

I stay up as late as I can, making more.

(Tally: 83)

Ophelia is bored watching me make stars →

Maybe I stay up too late, because my brain goes crazy in my dreams. I'm making ninja stars in my sleep.

Bright and early in the morning we go to the Able Athletes games. There must be a thousand people here. It's loud—CRAZY LOUD—with music on the loudspeakers and throngs of cheering people.

Mo's family and I check in at a table to get a list saying where to be at what time.

Holding hands to form a chain, we weave our way through the crowds to the volleyball gym.

Thomas plays at noon. My job (and Mo's) is to watch from the bleachers, cheer for all the athletes we see, and hug them when they're done playing.

We see other huggers giving balloons and flowers to some of the athletes. (No trophies.)

My face hurts from smiling so much.

And then I feel so filled up with emotion that my eyes start leaking.

Thomas fits in perfectly with everyone today. Here he isn't different. He's just another kid.

Thomas doesn't seem to be nervous before his game. He jumps up and down, cheering for the other athletes. When it's his turn to play, he smiles and tells us to watch. Mo is ready with her camera.

Thomas serves the ball over the net each time—maybe he plays volleyball better than I play soccer.

Mo and I cheer loudly:

Go, go, Thomas! Hit that ball!

Go, go, Thomas! You're so tall!

(Well, it's the best we can think of on the spot.)

Go, go, Thomas! Show the crowd!

Go, go, Thomas! We're so proud!

At the end of each game, all of the players on both teams hug one another. In soccer we just slap hands and say, "Good game." (And most of us probably don't even mean it.)

We get in line to hug Thomas and his teammates. Mo gives Thomas a new trophy that I am sure she made herself. It's really cool.

Thomas hugs Mo very tight.

I pull out the crown of ninja stars I've made and put it on Thomas's head.

He loves it! His eyes get wide. His hands fly up to feel it. His mouth has the most gargantuan smile I have ever seen.

He takes the crown off to examine. But then he starts taking it apart. Why??

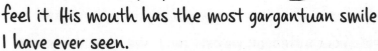

Ahhh, I see. He's giving a star to each of the other players! That means we need more fast!

I jump into action, asking, "Who has paper?" I'm about to use the blank pages in this book when Mo's mom pulls a magazine from her tote bag. It's perfect! I rip out pages for everyone around me. They make a few stars, and then they teach their friends how to make them.

Long chain of helpers

Within minutes we've made hundreds of colorful ninja stars from magazine paper (and a few from notebook paper too). We give the stars to the Able Athletes players around us—and in return we get hugs.

In the car on the way home, Mo makes two more stars:

I should wear these for Crazy Hair Day at school tomorrow.

Yay, Spirit Week!

Usually it's hard to crawl out of bed on Monday morning. Today I jump out of bed fast. It's Spirit Week! Crazy Hair Day specifically.

Risa volunteered to do my hair today. She puts a jade statue in it and makes my hair "cascade around it for a fountain effect."

I don't understand her words but I love the finished style. Josh likes it, too, and begs Risa to do the same hairstyle on him.

He wants green fountain hair but Mom vetoes that plan. I think Risa has a future in hairstyling.

Mom: Great job, Risa! Ellie, you're, um, beautiful. Josh, you have a lot of guts going to high school looking like that.

Josh: I'm hoping they take my photo for the yearbook.

Me: Mom, Mo wants pierced ears. I asked her mom if we could do it for Mo's birthday and she said yes. Will you go with us?

Josh: I can pierce them for her.

We all stare at Josh.

Me: Can we do it Thursday after soccer? (ignoring Josh)

Risa: How would you pierce Mo's ears? (NOT ignoring Josh)

Josh: Well, I've been improving my aim with my dartboard—

Me: Um, let me think about that for a sec. Okay, I'm done thinking. NO!!!!!!!!!!

Mom: Sure. I'll call Mo's mom.

Me: Thanks, Mom! And one more thing—please tell her mom we want to keep it a surprise for Mo.

I'm so excited about Mo's present that I run all the way to school. Hmm. Running is getting easier. I forget my hair looks weird until I walk in the school door and see all the surprised faces. I fit right in, though. We ALL look funny. Mo and I crack up when we first see each other.

Even the teachers are hilarious.

(Every day is Crazy Hair Day for some people)

We talk about Able Athletes at lunch. I tell the group about the trophy Mo made for Thomas.

Travis

Kev

Mo: I wish I could make trophies for all the kids at Able Athletes. They'd be so excited!

Me: They'd really appreciate them.

Travis: We could help you make some.

Mo: We'd need hundreds. Too many to make.

Kev: We could buy them.

Travis: So, you won the lottery recently?

Mo: Wait—we could have a fund-raiser, and then buy the trophies. But what would we sell?

Me: ART!! My drawings, your photos . . .

Travis: Hey, that could work! We could get the Journey group to help organize it!

Mo: It's a plan, Stan!

After lunch in Mr. Brendall's class we have another group project. I should have known when he passed out plastic gloves that it would be absolutely, totally, thoroughly, and completely disgusting. I don't even want to look at it.

On the other hand, it's kind of cool: dissecting an arrow squid!

The stink wakes up Ahmed, who asks if I forgot to wash my armpits today.

Ha, ha. (Not funny.)

Jamian pokes the squid to see if anything gross will squirt out.

I'm gonna throw up!

We're running out of time fooling around. I don't want to, but I start dissecting the thing.

Cut this. Find that. Move this. I think I'm doing a pretty good job. I find and label the beak, suction cups, head, two tentacles, and ink sac.

Jamian points out the obvious stuff: two eyeballs, two fins, and eight arms.

I ask Ahmed three times to count the hearts. (There are three.)

Finally it's time for the last section of the assignment, the fun part: drawing with squid ink!

Urp!

Suddenly Sitka snatches the scissors from my hand and pierces the ink sac. She dips the pen (a weird plasticky thing in the squid's back) into the ink and starts doodling.

pen   ink sac

Why does SHE get to draw with it first? She's been sitting back the whole time, and I've been doing the hard work, dealing with zombie squid.

I'm just about to grab the pen out of Sitka's hand when Mr. Brendall sneaks up behind us.

"I see you're cooperating and acting like a team. Nicely done, all of you!"

Sigh. Yeah. Cooperating just fine here.

When I'm really frustrated and it's socially unacceptable to throw myself on the floor and kick and scream (which is, um, pretty much my whole life ever since I was four), I get creative.

Today instead of throwing a tantrum, I develop these faces out of symbols and letters on the class computer. Then I make up a story to go with them:

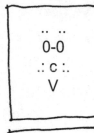 1. Robot Ellie is happy in science class.

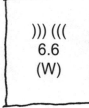 2. Along comes Medusa-haired evil zombie squid.

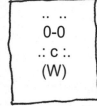 3. Robot Ellie turns into her own secret weapon: Vampire Robot Ellie!

 4. Medusa-haired evil zombie squid slithers away, crying.

In our Journey meeting we've just finished a puzzle when Ms. Trebuchet, the art teacher, comes in.

Travis mentions the art fund-raiser we want to do. Right then, Ms. Trebuchet whips out her phone, contacts Art of Art's Gallery, talks for a couple of minutes, and hangs up.

She announces we can have an art sale at the gallery on Friday. We tell her we don't have any art to sell yet! She says it's all arranged. If we want, we're to meet at the gallery tomorrow to create the art.

Of course, we're all in total shock. She handled the whole thing in, what, two minutes? Well, not the WHOLE thing. We still have to make a few thousand dollars' worth of art.

Ms. Trebuchet asks, "Does this work for all of you?"

I yell, "We'll MAKE it work!"

Our little art sale will be at a <u>real</u> art gallery! Wow. This will be so much bigger than I thought!

Miss Claire says this seems like an appropriate project for the Journey group because it's creative and it'll take organization skills.

To us, though, it sounds like pure fun: bring a few friends to the gallery tomorrow, paint pictures and make frames for them, hang it all on the walls, and invite everyone we know to come and see it and buy something.

Then we'll give the money to the people in charge of Able Athletes, and they'll buy the trophies.

When we're done jumping and dancing about the gallery show, Miss Claire continues with our Journey meeting. Today's challenge is team building. Not that we need it.

We start with ten people on a big blue tarp. Easy enough. Gradually Miss Claire reduces the size of the space. Pretty soon we're ten people squished onto a small concrete block.

The only way to keep from falling is to link arms or hug one another. Otherwise it's impossible.

Miss Claire says life is like that too—we're interdependent. No man is an island. I admit, this makes me feel a little better about group projects.

As usual, soccer follows the Journey meeting. But this time soccer feels different.

Mo and I work together, off to the side, while Dad is busy with the rest of the Mustangs. He says this is what I need most. I'm a little embarrassed, but I agree. Mo and I practice dribbling, passing the ball, and scoring (for the right goal, ahem). Maybe it'll pay off for the next game.

At night, I practice in our backyard by myself. I'm not an island. I'm a peninsula! Or a continent? Better than incontinent, as Josh would say.

Speaking of Josh, on Tuesday morning I open my bedroom door and a bag falls from the door. Confetti explodes all over my room, the stairs, and me. It's even in my mouth!

I walk downstairs, still piled with confetti.

Josh is in the kitchen, laughing like a hyena. I stand next to him and do my wet-dog imitation, shaking my head.

Confetti flies off of me and all over him.

The best part: Dad makes Josh clean it all up. I hug Dad and sit down for breakfast.

After breakfast I get dressed for Mix-Up Day at school, the second day of Spirit Week.
My family takes care of me.

Grandpa's party fez

Mom's scarf

Dad's necktie

Risa's frilly blouse

Josh's pants

Risa's toe shoe
(idea inspired by Ben-Ben's single bare foot)

I make Mo promise not to post my photo online. (I forget to ask her to promise not to print my photo, frame it, and hang it in the art gallery show tonight. Oops.)

Daquon likes my mismatched-shoe look and trades one of his shoes with Jamian. Pretty soon everyone is wearing two different shoes, like Mo and me. Ha! A new tradition!

Our families have been helping us spread the word about the gallery. And we tell everyone at school and everyone at soccer practice to come to Art's Gallery tonight to help with the Able Athletes Art Create-a-thon.

That's why Art's Gallery is super crowded. It's all friends, family, and friends of friends and family. I think people just like to have something to rally around. We get Risa to announce because she's good on stage.

Welcome! Thanks for coming to help Able Athletes! Now let's make some cool art!

Yay!

A bunch of us dismantle pallets that Mo's dad brought from his gas station.

The teachers and parents cut the pallet wood, sand the worst bits, then hammer pieces together to make picture frames.

We have 137 people here, and we're amazingly productive. We end up with 600 paintings! Plus a few flying dragon mobiles (made by me).

Practically everyone I know is here, including my soccer team and Mudslide (who, it turns out, is pretty creative with a paintbrush).

She traces a large outline of Thomas on a big sheet of paper. Then she fills in the drawing with happy colors. She calls it Thomas's Jubilant Shadow. It's abstract, completely different from the art I like to do, and it's FANTASTIC. Everyone agrees. Thomas loves it. Mudslide gets a long line of models to outline and paint next.

As we leave Art's Gallery, we're ALL jubilant.

The next morning I get up early because 1) it's
Wednesday, which means Breakfast Games! Yay!!
We play Simon Says while eating. It's not easy.
And 2) it's Teacher Twin Day at school.

This might be the only time in
the history of Ben-Ben that
he stands still for more than
a minute. I wish I had Mo's
camera. Usually in photos
Ben-Ben's just a blur.

I get to school and find a few of us had the same idea: dress as Ms. Trebuchet for Teacher Twin Day. Do I detect a tiny bit of a smile as she notices our outfits? Hmm. Maybe not.

Mo and Mr. Brendall are dressed like Mrs. Whittam. Travis and Mrs. Whittam are dressed like Mr. Brendall. Principal Ping doesn't seem to enjoy Teacher Twins. Maybe it's hard for her to figure out who the real teachers are!

At lunch there are teachers everywhere—so I'm surprised when Ryan starts something.

He's dressed like Mr. Brendall—maybe he feels powerful? Ryan flicks a french fry at Kevin. It gets flicked around the room. When it comes back to Ryan, he flicks TWO french fries. And then he flicks all the food on his tray.

Glenda is dressed like Principal Ping and gives him detention. Then we ALL do. Then the REAL Principal Ping walks in and gives Ryan detention for real. Everybody laughs, even Ryan! Principal Ping looks stunned. She obviously doesn't know that "she" (Glenda) already gave him detention.

In the afternoon we play spongeball.

Spongeball Rules

1. Divide into two teams.
   Use a squishy foam ball.

2. The first team has one
   chance to throw the ball
   at the other team, trying
   to hit someone. Whoever gets hit by the ball is
   out of the game.
      If the player isn't hit but instead catches the
   ball, the thrower is out.

3. Next it's the other team's
   chance to throw the ball
   and get a player out.

4. The winner is the team
   who gets all of its
   opponents out.

Everyone's cracking up. How can you stay
serious when a foamy ball hits your ankle with all
the force of a butterfly?

Every time Mr. Brendall
hits someone he says,
"TAKE THAT, Ms.
Trebuchet!" (Or
Mr. Lopez,
Principal Ping,
Mrs. Whittam,
or whoever
the student
dressed like a
teacher is.)

My strategy: hide
behind all the best
players. I'm out
eventually, but I'm
not the first
one out.

After school we have a Journey meeting. Ms. Trebuchet gives a quick guest presentation about Rube Goldberg. He made cartoons of convoluted, silly contraptions with lots of complicated steps that eventually perform a simple task.

To illustrate, Ms. Trebuchet opens a big box and arranges the contents onto numbered dots on the floor. Then she makes the contraption work.

Croquet mallet hits a ball into series of books.

They topple into a bowling pin, which makes a golf ball fly into a ruler in a cup, which nudges a bowling ball down a ramp.

This flattens a paper-doll row.

The dolls pivot a Styrofoam cup that expels a ball that hits a block that moves a ruler enough to drop a magnet onto a book that has a steel plate lying under a page. The magnets join, creating a bookmark.

Okay, my first reaction is that this is insane. But insanity and genius are closely connected. Just look at Albert Einstein's hair.

Miss Claire assigns a "human" Rube Goldberg contraption. First we each think of some sort of motion we can do to move a beach ball. We draw our ideas on paper. We arrange the ideas in sequence. Then we arrange ourselves physically—and actually do those moves! It takes many tries to get it right. But when it's right, it's magical. We don't want to stop!

1. batter
2. lifter
3. tipper
4. smacker
5. pusher
6. stopper
7. puller
8. redirector
9. kicker
10. aimer
me

It's seriously awesome.

Miss Claire has one more example of a Rube Goldberg contraption, a marble-racing game. While we set it up, she tells us that Rube Goldberg is the theme of the Journey Tournament on Saturday.

That's in three days—barely enough time to panic! But Miss Claire says we already have the best tools possible: our brains.

The best way to prepare is to get plenty of sleep, eat right, and show up on time. We'll need every Journey member, so nobody's allowed to get sick or hurt.

Travis   Yasmeen   Glenda   Mo

Kwanita   Ryan   Kev

Bae   Daquon   Me   Miss Claire

Our Team on Normal Hair Day

We have just enough time after Journey to get home, gobble down a snack, change clothes, and fix our teacher hair to look normal before soccer practice starts. All this rushing around makes me even more nervous about Journey Tourney. We have two soccer games the same day. Can we do it all?

Mo has a plan: "As soon as the second game ends, we'll race home, change clothes, and drive to the Journey Tourney. We'll even be fifteen minutes early."

I ask if soccer games ever run late.

Mo says, "Hardly ever."

Morning good! It's Yadsruht and Backward Day at school. I want Dad to give me a ride to school by driving in reverse.

No, you have to klaw.

Klaw?? Oh! Walk, backward!

I walk to school, but in the hallways we klaw. For today, Mo is Om. Travis is Sivart. I am Eille, Glenda is Adnelg. Just using your friend's name is suddenly lots of fun!

In English (Hsilgne) class we read graphic novels from Japan. They start at the back of the book and read from right to left, instead of from left to right. I ♡ the art.

Srm. Mattihw issues a challenge: extra points to whoever can sing the alphabet backward.

Most of us get to about T and drop out.
One kid is left standing all the way back to A: Sivart
(who by the way has his clothes on backward).

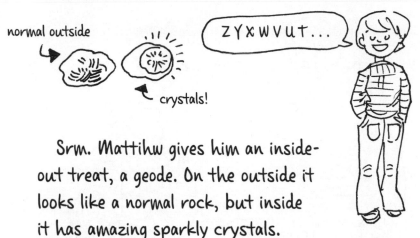

normal outside

crystals!

ZYXWVUT...

Srm. Mattihw gives him an inside-
out treat, a geode. On the outside it
looks like a normal rock, but inside
it has amazing sparkly crystals.

Right before lunch we play with palindromes,
words or phrases that read the same both
forward and backward.

- Hanna
- Bob
- noon
- Madam, I'm Adam.
- A man, a plan, a canal: Panama.
  I think of two:
- Yo, banana boy! ← Josh calling the fruit server.
- Rats! Llama'll star! ← Alpaca, upset because
the llama got the lead role in the school play.

Of course at lunch we eat dessert first. Ryan spits out food instead of eating it. It's totally gross but everyone laughs.

I learn a few useful words today. Hehehe.

Good news: this is our last day of group projects in science. Bad news: my group is just as dysfunctional as ever, and it's starting to affect my grade in this class. I have to make this work.

Our assignment is to see the human heart as a system inside a bigger system, compare it to something else we know about, and write and illustrate our ideas. I start with Plan A:

Time for Plan B:

Me: It's Backward Day. One of you should take over and run this group.

::crickets chirping::

Ahmed: Wake me up when this is over.

Me: No, wait! Don't nap! I have another plan!

(But I don't, really. Think fast, Eille . . .)

Ahmed: Do you have to go on and on? You're keeping me awake.

Me: Yes! That's what a heart does. Day and night, on and on.

Jamian: Mr. Brendall took my cell phone.

Me: Hey, cell phones are like brain cells! They communicate with the heart and tell it to speed up or slow down.

Sitka's looking out the window where our school custodian is working.

Sitka: Look! Mr. Rogers found something dead. Eww.

Me: The heart's like Mr. Rogers, removing stuff we don't need! Or wait, is that the liver?

I'm stuck. Maybe I do deserve a bad grade in this class.

Suddenly Sitka bursts into action.

Sitka: Mr. Rogers is like a heart! He's the heart of our school. Everyone loves him. He moves things, he cleans things, he fixes things. Maybe we can draw a heart with tiny Mr. Rogerses inside it, moving valves and pumping and stuff.

She starts drawing. I watch, in shock. Ahmed and Jamian actually start helping. We all add to the poster. I must admit, it's really cool when it's done.

Mr. Brendall catches me on the way out of the classroom. "Good, solid job, Ellie. That was a unique way to solve the problem."

Grade: A!

"Actually, it was mostly Sitka," I tell him.

On the way home I am thinking the birds are singing extra pretty. The flowers are especially bright. And wasn't Mr. Brendall uncomfortable all day with his shirt on backward??

I notice in soccer practice I'm getting better at controlling the ball, thanks to Mo's help. I'm excited about her birthday present: Mom and I are taking Mo and her mom to get Mo's ears pierced and out for dinner—TONIGHT!!!!

Mo has NO idea. What she especially doesn't know is how hard it's been to keep all of this a secret from her! I hang out with Mo most of the day, every day.

What did you get me for my birthday tomorrow?

Ohhh, your birthday is tomorrow?

Want a goat? Or is that a baaad idea? Heh heh heh.

After soccer practice I take a quick shower and grab the birthday card I made for Mo. Then Mom and I go pick up Mo and her mom. Mo still has NO clue what's going on!

We drive to All Ears. Mo thinks her mom just wants to get a pair of earrings. Walking in the door, we spring it on her: we're here to get her ears pierced. And—Mom says—mine too!

There's just one little problem. Mo wants me to go first. This way, if it hurts too much, Mo will get a necklace instead.

There's no chickening out for me. Yikes.

The saleslady gives me a choice: one at a time or both at once? I choose one at a time.

When the first earring shoots through my ear I want to scream and run and leave my second ear unpierced. Nothing wrong with the one-pierced-ear pirate look.

The second earring zings through my earlobe. I almost faint. I tell Mo we can get her something else instead of pierced ears. (I don't want to hurt her.)

But Mo is brave. She gets both ears pierced at the same time, and the only sound is a happy "Squee!!!!"

In the end, it was worth it. Mo and I love our new earrings!

We're reminded not to take them out for six weeks and to keep them clean. Mo gives me a hug and says this is the very best present ever!

Then we go out to dinner—with birthday cake for dessert. We sing "Happy Birthday" loud and off-key, but Mo doesn't embarrass easily.

At home, as I get ready for bed and turn my new earrings three times and dot them with

"Happy New Ears"

special pierced-earring solution, I think about Mo. Today was fun but it wasn't the end of her birthday surprises from me.

I have a plan for tomorrow.

Friday at school is Silence Is Golden Day and that means NO speaking for the entire day. I never knew being silent could be so hilarious.

Mo and I dress as mimes.

imaginary box around us

Now I see why we've been studying American Sign Language in Mrs. Whittam's class: so we can talk with our hands. There's a lot of note passing too. All of this means it takes a long time to have a short conversation.

In English we watch a silent movie, take a test on Greek mythology, and start learning Morse code.

At lunch we wave to Glenda, who has taped
her mouth shut to make it easier to not talk.
(Everyone knows what a nonstop talker Glenda is!)
Travis drops his tray accidentally.

C R A S H ! ! ! !

It echoes through
the silent cafeteria.
We laugh hysterically—
and silently. It's funny
how much you can say
without speaking.

On Travis's tray
was a cupcake for
Mo. It's the only thing
that survives the fall.

Travis hands his cupcake to Mo and I realize this is the perfect time for Mo's next birthday surprise.

I climb onto a chair. People stare—this is not something I would normally do. I can see grim Principal Ping start toward me, but she stops. I proceed.

I wave my arms so everyone is looking at me. I point at Mo.

I hold my hands up and sign:

M O

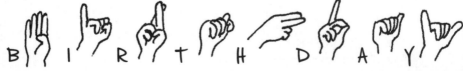

B I R T H D A Y

American Sign Language symbol for music

Everyone nods. I count down: three, two, one. Then holding up my arms like a concert conductor, I make exaggerated motions and mouth the words.

The whole cafeteria (Principal Ping included) sings a silent "Happy Birthday" to Mo. Everyone's laughing. I could almost hear the screechy singing.

(Nothing. It's absolutely silent.)

Mo hugs me.

After school we have soccer practice as usual. Tomorrow we have two games so we work out extra hard today.

Crunches crunch your belly and turn your legs to jelly.

Push-ups hurt my arms and chest. I like the part when I can rest.

Galloping, trotting, sprinting, jogging: running laps makes me want to take naps.

Finally, the good part of practice: playing together on the field. Our hard work is paying off! I think we might even win a game tomorrow. Maybe both games? Dare we hope?

At the end of practice, the whole team sings "Happy Birthday" to Mo (out loud this time!).

Mo and I remind everyone about the Art's Gallery sale tonight.

Bring your friends!

Support Able Athletes!

Come see Mudslide's art!

We've been spreading the word, but will people come?

They do! Our gallery show is a HUGE, crowded success! Every person I know is here. It's amazing how much better the art looks when it's framed. Kind of like how uniforms dress up a team.

Thomas is showing everyone the art that he made. We're all proud of him.

We take the soccer snack idea from the slumber party and make it more art-ish.

◄— peanut butter cracker with a fruity face
(Dad says stick with your strengths.)

We sell so much art that even Art, the gallery owner, is surprised. He says, "Anytime you kids want to do a fund-raiser for a worthy cause, let me know."

You're the girl who made the stars at the meet!

The Able Athletes board of advisors thanks us for the money we raised. They say it's enough for trophies for TWO years!

As the gallery is closing, I hug Miss Claire.

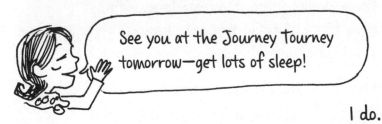

See you at the Journey Tourney tomorrow—get lots of sleep!

I do.

Dad wakes me up early in the morning. For a second I think it must be Wednesday, but it's the BIG day: two soccer games and Journey Tourney. But first, breakfast. My whole family is up, which is strange for a Saturday. Josh is making omelets to order.

Mom pours juice. Dad made muffins.

Risa has a riddle: "What's blue and smells like red paint?"

Ben-Ben uses his spatula to swat at a grape on the table. It wobble-rolls over to my plate.

(blue paint)

Josh hands me a slotted spoon. I nudge the grape back to Ben-Ben. It comes back. I swat at it, aiming carefully this time. Mom sits down with an ice cream scoop. Risa grabs a ladle. Dad picks a wooden spoon. And thus we invent the rollicking game of Kitchen Tool Hockey.

Somehow extra grapes fly into the game. We make up rules: If a grape lands on your plate you get a point. If a grape lands on the floor you get two points. The lowest score wins.

In the middle of the game Josh starts chanting:

Ellie, Ellie, it's your big day!

As your family, we want to say:

We'll be there to cheer for your teams,

Soccer games and Rube Goldberg schemes!

I'm not nervous at all anymore. I'm hyped up for victory. We head to the soccer field.

As usual, before the game both teams line up while the ref inspects for disqualifying stuff. He calls out untied shoelaces, glittery hair clips, bracelets, and untucked shirts. He stops at Mo and me. "Remove the jewelry."

What? Remove? Earrings aren't jewelry! They're, um . . .

"We can't!" we protest. "The piercings will close!"

The ref starts telling Dad a horror story about earrings in a high school game.

Mudslide interrupts. "Excuse me, sir. My old coach let us put tape on our earrings. Could they try that?"

Huh. Mudslide to the rescue.

gobs of tape

On the field I pay serious attention to the ball and which goal is ours. I rehearse scoring and assisting goals in my head, over and over.

On the bench I cheer until I am almost hoarse, and I get everyone else to cheer too. I give song suggestions to Josh's kazoo band. I make quick signs for the bleachers fans to hold up.

Flip them down:

Mudslide, er, Victoria, scores three goals.

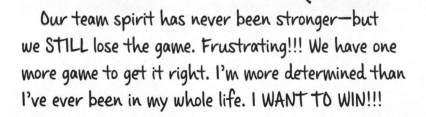

Yay, Vic-SCORE-ia!

Our team spirit has never been stronger—but we STILL lose the game. Frustrating!!! We have one more game to get it right. I'm more determined than I've ever been in my whole life. I WANT TO WIN!!!

Game 2: The first half speeds by. Before we know it, there are just three minutes until the end of the game. The score is tied, 4 to 4, when suddenly the ball comes right to me!

Mudslide is nearby. Sparkle and Toni are in front of me. I have a clear shot at the goal!

But just as I am lining myself up, I hear someone scream.

I twist around and see Victoria standing still with a weird look on her face. I look for Dad or the ref just as someone kicks the ball away from me.

I rush to Victoria and help her limp to the sidelines.

Almost there. Keep going. You can do it.
Almost there. Keep going. You can do it.

Whistles blow. Dad gets Victoria to the bench. Her face is distorted and she's crying quietly now. She's in <u>serious</u> pain. My stomach starts to hurt in sympathy.

The whistles blow again. Applause erupts from the spectators. It's the end of the game. Judging by my friends' faces, we lost.

Oh no! The other team must have gotten the ball and scored while Victoria and I were down.

Half of my team rushes to Victoria. The other half rushes to me. I expect everyone to yell at me for wrecking the game. I had a clear shot at the goal. Instead:

"You did the right thing."

"There will be other games."

"I'm glad you stepped in to help Victoria."

"Way to go."

Wow, I have a great team!

Victoria's ankle is starting to swell. Dad wraps it and ices it. Then he gets on the phone with Victoria's parents.

I'm trying to cheer up Victoria with the riddle about paint when Risa grabs my arm and says we have to run or I'll be late for the Journey Tourney. Yikes!! I forgot all about it!

Dad will stay with Victoria until her parents come. Mo's family left twenty minutes ago. If Risa and I don't leave right this second, we'll never make it. And we're off.

Risa's boyfriend, Peter, drives, taking every shortcut he can to avoid construction traffic. It doesn't work.

We're stuck in traffic a mile from the arena. We sit there. And sit there . . . Risa looks at me.

Risa: Think you can run?

Me: Ulp! Yes?

Risa: Let's go!

As we huff and puff up the steps of the arena, Mom shoves a sandwich in my hand. Miss Claire grabs my other hand.

We zigzag through the hallways and FINALLY . . .

. . . I'm in the right place.

The arena is cavernous. Twenty nervous-looking groups will compete. The announcer tells the audience to take their seats, so I head for my team.

The Journey Tourney begins. Our challenge: demonstrate the path to world peace using the Rube Goldberg theme. We have four hours!

The announcer says, "Have fun with it. Silliness counts. Okay, go!"

My team gathers around a table to brainstorm. What brings people together in peace? Love, festivals, computers, parties, elections, a common cause, concerts, sports, the Olympics. We write down every idea, no matter how big or small.

We work like a machine: brainstorm, discuss, compromise, plan. No voice goes unheard.

Although some of our details are sketchy, after a while we have enough figured out to start construction.

And we've decided on our theme: the Olympics.

Eight of us will make mini contraptions, each based on an Olympic sport. Travis and Kev will make sure all of the contraptions work.

We decide to make our big contraption in a pie shape with eight slices for eight sports. The circle in the middle stands for the world. We'll work in some peace signs somewhere, and maybe confetti.

Mo picks volleyball in honor of Thomas. I pick soccer, the #1 sport in the world. Here's my plan: kicker (A) knocks over book players (B), sending ball off teeter-totter (C), down chute (D), into cup (E), shoots over to player (F), who pivots to kick ball (G) into paper goal (H), which flips open to release marbles (I) to center world (J)—where they meet marbles from all of the other sports pie slices at the same time! It'll be phenomenal!

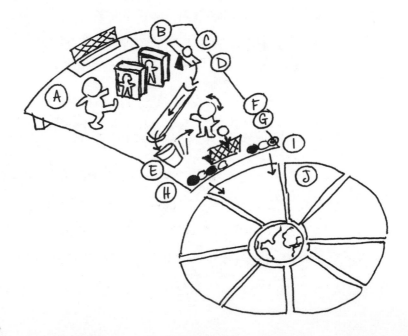

We map out our pie slices. Then we visit the giant pile of props in the arena center to get the supplies and tools we'll need to make this thing work.

It isn't really a fun project yet, and it isn't silly. But it's going okay, I think. I try to stay focused.

The audience comes and goes. We get free snacks.

Four hours fly by a lot faster than you'd think. The warning buzzer signals that we have ten minutes to finish. We step back, evaluate our contraption, and make a few quick changes. Then we get ready to show it off to the judges.

The audience applauds as each team steps up to the microphone in turn to demonstrate their contraptions. They're all different. Some are really cool.

When it's my school's turn, Travis describes our vision to the audience while each of us starts our part of the contraption, our piece of the pie, at the same time.

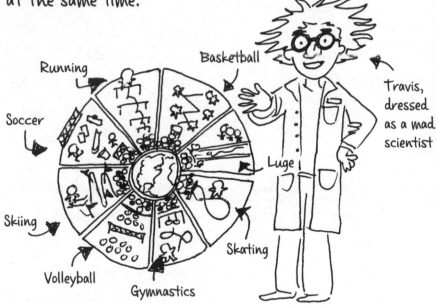

Running

Basketball

Soccer

Luge

Travis, dressed as a mad scientist

Skiing

Skating

Volleyball

Gymnastics

It's rough. Some levers malfunction and some marbles get stuck. We use a yardstick to nudge them into action. Most of the marbles never make it to the center part, the world. Confetti doesn't fly up at the end. My throat feels lumpy.

Peace sign with dominoes.

How to grow world peas.

Stiff competition.

Go Mo + Team!

Thomas's sign

Dad and Mom's sign

Our minute in the spotlight ends quickly. I look for people I know in the audience. Josh brought his kazoo band. Risa, Victoria, and Travis's sisters have pom-poms. Thomas made a sign for us. Mo's dad has her camera—the flash goes off a million times.

Mom and Dad are sitting next to each other, giving me the "I love you" sign.

I flash the same sign back to them, and then see the most amazing sight: instantly "I love you" hands go up everywhere. Dozens, hundreds, a thousand people are flashing sign language "I love yous"—not just to me, but to all of us on the arena floor.

I feel like I just won!

The judges are ready to announce the scores. I tell myself to do yoga breathing to calm down, but I'm too excited to listen to myself!

My team grips hands, standing next to our contraption. Third place is announced, and it's not us.

the third-place winners

their awesome new trophy ➤

I stop listening. I had been hoping for third. Now I'm just thinking about how cool my team is and how fun Journey has been. Challenging but fun.

"Pssst! Better luck next year!"

Suddenly my team goes crazy, jumping up and down. We won SECOND PLACE!!!!!!!!!! Our families and friends are yelling and jumping too.

We win custody of this amazingly cool trophy for one year:

The first-place trophy? That goes to a group that included all sorts of oddball stuff in their contraption—boots, clocks, chickens (cutouts of them, not real ones). They did a great job. They deserve to win first prize.

After everyone hugs, Miss Claire tells us that my mom and dad offered our yard for a team celebration picnic tomorrow. It'll be the perfect end to our Journey season.

Eventually the Journey Tourney crowds go home, and so does my family. I'm ravenously hungry! Dad says he's glad because we have one more event.

Dad had promised pizza if our soccer team won its games. Even though we didn't win, Dad says we showed winning attitudes and outstanding sportsmanship on the field today. So pizza it is!

Everyone meets at our favorite pizza parlor. Even Victoria is there—on crutches. Her ankle will heal nicely, but not soon. Dad offers her a job as the Mustangs' assistant coach.

She takes it! (I'm a little nervous. I know she's going to make me work hard.)

Halfway through dinner, Dad taps his fork against his water glass to get everyone's attention. He says he and Victoria have chosen the Most Valuable Player of the day . . .

It's me!!! Dad gives me a new sketchbook. The best part is this:

Mo presents me with one of her special trophies made just for the occasion.

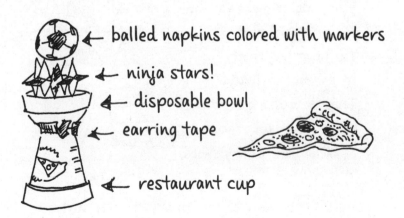

← balled napkins colored with markers

← ninja stars!

← disposable bowl

← earring tape

← restaurant cup

I laugh and so does everybody else. Mo rocks.

Happy Henry

At home that night Dad and Mom tell me they're proud of me. Risa says I can borrow anything I want of hers for one full day. Ben-Ben challenges me to a game of Spatula—Brussels Sprouts Ball. We keep losing the ball. Mom makes us substitute a Ping-Pong ball. Henry won't eat that.

Josh sings the song he wrote for me.

Ellie, sports make you smelly.
But in your heart
You have the start
Of courage and guts
Though you're quite a klutz.
We're all proud of you
So clean your stinky shoes.

I resist the temptation to point out that, technically, "you" and "shoes" don't rhyme.
I go to sleep smiling.

The next day is party day! We scramble to clean up the house. Honestly, I think Josh and Ben-Ben make more work, but they do have a very well-developed sense of fun.

Sponge shoes scrub the picnic tables and then the floors →

My Journey teammates and their families arrive and help put tablecloths on tables and haul chairs to the yard. Dad fires up the grill. Daquon kicks up the Hacky Sack—which is a lot easier to control than a soccer ball.

But I still stink at it.

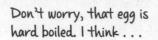

Don't worry, that egg is hard boiled. I think . . .

Ben-Ben makes his own fun playing Spatula-Egg Ball.

Miss Claire says she wants to bring our Journey Tourney project to the library to display with the second-place trophy. Yay! That makes us kind of famous, doesn't it?

Kev wants to get started on the next Journey Tourney season right away.

Miss Claire says for now we should celebrate our success, enjoy our families and friends, and have fun. I agree. I've been way too busy. I need a break! The soccer season isn't over yet.

Speaking of soccer, Travis suggests a giant game of soccer with twenty people on each team. I notice Victoria's smile fades. So instead I propose a game of Balloon Bobble.

Ben-Ben was here

This is the perfect game for a crowd.

When the balloons have all popped, we make ninja stars and practice our aim, boys against the girls, until it's too dark to see.

Then we gaze at the real stars

and feel

real

peace.

ACKNOWLEDGMENTS

Thank you to these most valuable players: my family; Carrie and Sierra Pearson; Anne, Ben, Isaac, and Zachary Thelander; Diane Ross Allen; Karen Jones Lee; Tam Smith; Paul and Lindsey LaForest; and the girls' volleyball team, coaches, parents, and refs at Gardner Middle School.

RUTH McNALLY BARSHAW, lifelong writer and artist, has worked in the advertising field, illustrated for newspapers, and won numerous essay-writing contests. She lives in Lansing, Michigan, with her family. Visit her at www.ruthexpress.com.